READ MORE ABOUT
Basil's adventures!

THE GREAT MOUSE DETECTIVE

BOOK 8

Basil and the Library Ghost

CREATED BY *Eve Titus* WRITTEN BY *Cathy Hapka*

ILLUSTRATED BY *David Mottram*

ALADDIN
NEW YORK LONDON TORONTO SYDNEY NEW DELHI

This book is a work of fiction. Any references to historical events, real people, or real places are used fictitiously. Other names, characters, places, and events are products of the author's imagination, and any resemblance to actual events or places or persons, living or dead, is entirely coincidental.

ALADDIN

An imprint of Simon & Schuster Children's Publishing Division
1230 Avenue of the Americas, New York, New York 10020
First Aladdin paperback edition May 2020
Text copyright © 2020 by Estate of Eve Titus
Illustrations copyright © 2020 by David Mottram
Also available in an Aladdin hardcover edition.

For information about special discounts for bulk purchases, please contact Simon & Schuster Special Sales at 1-866-506-1949 or business@simonandschuster.com.
The Simon & Schuster Speakers Bureau can bring authors to your live event.
For more information or to book an event contact the Simon & Schuster Speakers Bureau at 1-866-248-3049 or visit our website at www.simonspeakers.com.
Cover designed by Karin Paprocki
Interior designed by Mike Rosamilia and Hilary Zarycky
The text of this book was set in Perpetua.
Manufactured in the United States of America 0221 OFF
2 4 6 8 10 9 7 5 3
Library of Congress Cataloging-in-Publication Data
Names: Hapka, Cathy, author. | Mottram, Dave, illustrator. | Titus, Eve, creator.
Title: Basil and the library ghost / created by Eve Titus ;
written by Cathy Hapka ; illustrated by David Mottram.
Description: First Aladdin hardcover/paperback edition. |
New York : Aladdin Books, 2020. | Series: The great mouse detective ; book 8 |
Audience: Ages 6 to 9. | Audience: Grades 2-3. |
Summary: When Basil of Baker Street and Dr. Dawson reunite with old friends, the C for Cheese Gang, at Oxford, they investigate rumors that Ratcliffe College's library is haunted.
Identifiers: LCCN 2019026966 (print) | LCCN 2019026967 (eBook) |
ISBN 9781534418653 (paperback) | ISBN 9781534418660 (hardcover) |
ISBN 9781534418677 (eBook)
Subjects: CYAC: Mice—Fiction. | Ghosts—Fiction. | Libraries—Fiction. |
Mystery and detective stories.
Classification: LCC PZ7.H1996 Basl 2020 (print) | LCC PZ7.H1996 (eBook) | DDC [Fic]—dc23
LC record available at https://lccn.loc.gov/2019026966
LC eBook record available at https://lccn.loc.gov/2019026967

Cast of Characters

BASIL	*English mouse detective*
DR. DAWSON	*his friend and associate*
ALFIE	*a shabby but friendly young mouse*
DR. RUPERT KERR	*Ratcliffe professor and dear old friend*
CLIVE	*a member of the C for Cheese Gang*
CEDRIC	*a member of the C for Cheese Gang*
CYRIL	*a member of the C for Cheese Gang*
LEWIS	*librarian*
PROFESSOR RATIGAN	*a much-discussed prison escapee*

VARIOUS STUDENTS, PROFESSORS, ALUMNI, AND OTHERS

Contents

1

AWAY TO OXFORD

WHEN MY DEAR FRIEND BASIL OF BAKER STREET and I set off for our university reunion, who could have guessed what adventure would greet us at dear old Ratcliffe College along with our old chums? Then again, when one is the most famous detective in all of mousedom, as Basil undeniably is, mysteries seem to follow one everywhere. . . .

But I'm getting ahead of myself. It all began one pleasant, sunny day. . . .

"Ah, the train," Basil commented, leaning forward to gaze out the top part of the window, which we could just see from our comfortable perch atop the luggage rack, well out of sight of

1

the human passengers below. "It's certainly the most modern and comfortable way to travel, is it not, Dawson?"

"Better than slow and smelly carriages indeed," I agreed, helping myself to another bite of the cheddar I'd brought as a snack. "And far better than going afoot, especially for such a great distance!"

"It's no wonder Mr. Sherlock Holmes travels so frequently by way of the Great Iron Horse," Basil mused, shaking his head in an admiring way.

I merely smiled at that. Sherlock Holmes is Basil's hero. In fact, he might well be considered the true founder of the mouse town of Holmestead, located in the basement of Basil's home at 221B Baker Street, despite the fact that the man had no idea the place existed! You see, many years earlier, Basil had dragged me along with some frequency to hide in Mr. Holmes's study and listen to his discussions with his friend Dr. Watson. However, getting there made for quite a harrowing journey across London from where we were then living.

But that seems ancient history by now. At the time of our current adventure, Basil and I had long since been settled in Holmestead, able to scurry upstairs to visit the great man's study as frequently as we desired. In that way, Basil had picked up even more tips and tricks of scientific sleuthing, which he had used to solve many crimes and become renowned throughout mousedom.

Little did we know as we rode across the countryside in comfort, heading to our reunion, that he would need to make use of his skills again so soon. . . .

"How much longer until we arrive in Oxford, Basil?" I asked, peering out the window. Outside, the crowded streets of London had long since given way to bucolic country vistas.

"Not long." Basil sounded distracted. He had just pulled out the copy of the *Mouse Times* he'd picked up at Paddington Station. "I do still wonder if I shouldn't have stayed in London, given the latest news."

I peered over his shoulder at the newspaper's headline: RATIGAN AND ACCOMPLICE ESCAPE NEWGATE PRISON.

It was troubling news indeed. Professor Ratigan was the most infamous criminal in mousedom—and Basil's archnemesis. He had been locked away in the mouse prison located within the walls of the notorious

Newgate ever since the last time Basil had foiled his nefarious plans and turned him over to the authorities.

"If Ratigan has any sense, he'll leave London immediately," I pointed out. "After all, you were the one who sent him to prison—again. Why would he remain in your home city, knowing you would be sure to come after him at once?"

Basil shrugged one thin shoulder. "Why do criminals commit any of their dastardly deeds?" he commented philosophically. Then he sighed and rubbed his whiskers. "Perhaps it's not too late to catch the next train back to London. . . ."

"Basil, you cannot!" I exclaimed. "Rupert asked specially for you to attend this reunion, did he not?"

"He did." Basil nodded thoughtfully. "He said he had something important and fascinating to discuss with me."

Dr. Rupert Kerr was an old school chum, a classmate of Basil's and mine at Ratcliffe. These days, he was a well-respected professor of mouse history and philosophy at that same esteemed institution.

Basil still looked thoughtful. "However, I expect Rupert would understand if I didn't make it," he said. "As you mentioned, I was the one who captured Ratigan, and I should be there now that he has broken free to create more mayhem."

Suddenly a whiskered face popped into view from behind a leather valise. "Begging your pardon, sirs," the stranger said with a respectful head bob. "I couldn't help but overhear your discussion." His curious black eyes turned toward Basil. "Could you really be the famous Basil of Baker Street?"

TRAVELING
COMPANIONSHIP

I WAS SO STARTLED BY THE YOUNG MOUSE'S
sudden appearance that I was unable to respond
for a moment. Ever since boarding, I'd assumed
that Basil and I had the luggage rack to ourselves.
But it seemed another mouse had been hidden
there all along!

Basil, luckily, retained his composure as usual.
"At your service, young sir," he said, bowing to
the younger mouse. "I am indeed Basil of Baker
Street. As to my fame, I shall leave that for others
to determine."

"Oh, what an honor!" the stranger exclaimed,
climbing over the valise to shake Basil's paw. "My

name is Alfie. I'm a big fan of your work, sir! Why, the way you nabbed that scoundrel Ratigan recently—unfortunate about his escape, eh? Why, I heard he'd been gone three hours before the guards noticed!"

"Did you?" Basil cocked a curious ear at him. "Where did you hear such a thing? It's not mentioned in the newspaper."

7

"Isn't it?" Alfie shrugged. "I overheard a pair of mice discussing it at the station while waiting to board. Perhaps it's merely a rumor. But never mind—the important thing is the masterful way you toppled Ratigan from his reign as the terror of mousedom. . . ."

He babbled on for another several moments, seeming quite familiar with Basil's exploits. Finally I interrupted by reaching out and taking his paw myself, giving it a hearty shake.

"And I am Dr. David Q. Dawson, Basil's friend

and travel companion," I said. "Young Alfie, what carries you to Oxford this fine day?"

Alfie bowed to me as well. "I'm hoping to find work there, sir," he explained. "And perhaps, one day . . ." He allowed his voice to trail off, his expression suddenly bashful.

"Perhaps one day what?" I asked.

Basil cocked his head. "Unless I miss my guess, you hope to study at Ratcliffe College—is that correct, Alfie?"

Alfie's eyes widened. "You guess correctly, sir," he exclaimed. Then he ducked his head. "But it might never happen."

"I'm impressed by your courage, young sir," I told him. "Not many mice would be brave enough to move to a new city with no job and nowhere to stay. . . ."

"Ah, but there I am lucky, for I have cousins in Oxford," Alfie said. Then he shook his head. "But enough about me! Please, if I might be so bold, what brings the great detective and his fine friend to Oxford? Could it be a fascinating and difficult mystery needing to be solved?"

"Nothing like that," I said with a chuckle. "Basil

and I are on a pleasure trip for once—on our way to a reunion with some university chums."

"That is correct." Basil blinked at the lad. "Surely you overheard us discussing that along with the rest of our conversation, young Alfie?"

Alfie looked sheepish, turning away and picking at a loose thread on the valise behind him. "I was not listening for very long," he said. "I fell asleep promptly upon boarding the train, and only awoke to hear your conversation for a few moments before I emerged just now. A reunion, you say?"

I sensed that the lad was trying to change the subject, perhaps embarrassed by the implication of eavesdropping. "Yes indeed," I responded before Basil could say another word. As the world's greatest detective, he sometimes forgets that there is no need to interrogate every mouse one meets! "It will be a pleasure to revisit our halcyon days of exams and exploits, eh, Basil?"

"I suppose so." Basil's gaze drifted momentarily to the newspaper, but then he shrugged. "It will be good to see our old school chums again, in any case."

"I've never been to Ratcliffe—or Oxford, for that matter," Alfie said. "Is it as big as London?"

The question made Basil chuckle. "Not nearly so," he replied. "But it is quite a bustling place in its own right. Of course, the university is at the center of life there—that would be the University of Oxford, founded at the dawn of this millennium and attended by many great and learned men since, from the great explorer Sir Walter Raleigh to the poet Percy Bysshe Shelley."

I nodded. "Ratcliffe College has a long and storied history as well," I told the younger mouse. "It seems natural that a fine mouse institution should rise up in the walls and baseboards of such an acclaimed human one. But it was only in the last century that Ratcliffe moved to its current location within the curious round building known as the Radcliffe Camera."

From there, we passed the rest of the time in companionable talk. Basil and I reminisced about our old school adventures, while Alfie asked numerous questions about our time at Ratcliffe, the layout of the town and the university, and lastly, about the

friends we would be visiting there this week.

"That gives me a thought, Alfie," I said, interrupting my own description of our friend Rupert. "Dr. Rupert Kerr has been at Ratcliffe for many years and is well connected there. If

Basil and I put in a word for you with him, he can surely help you find work."

"Thank you, sir. That would be most generous." Alfie gestured toward the window. "But look—it appears we're nearly there!"

BACK TO
SCHOOL

YOUNG ALFIE WAS RIGHT. WHEN I GLANCED OUT the window, I saw that the train was approaching our destination. Moments later Basil, Alfie, and I were scurrying across the platform to the shadow of a bench. There, we found a familiar figure awaiting us.

"Basil! Dawson!" came the cry from our friend Dr. Rupert Kerr. "You made it! When I saw the news about Ratigan in the morning paper, I was afraid . . . well, never mind!" He chuckled. "Even a great detective needs a day off now and then, eh, Basil?"

He elbowed Basil, who looked slightly sour. "I'm

not so sure about that, old friend," Basil said. "But I suppose there's no turning back now." He glanced toward the train, which was slowly moving off again.

"That's right." I patted Basil on the arm, then smiled at Rupert. "We're glad to be here! Where are the others?"

"Do you mean the C for Cheese Gang?" Rupert chuckled. "They're waiting for us back at Ratcliffe with cheese and drink."

"Wonderful." My stomach grumbled at the thought of cheese, for that cheddar snack seemed very long ago by then. "Ah, but before we go, allow me to introduce . . ."

My words trailed off as I glanced around and noticed that young Alfie was nowhere to be seen. Basil looked around too.

"Where did that lad go?" he said. "Odd for him to disappear just like that."

I shrugged. "Never mind. He probably became separated in the hubbub. I'm sure he'll turn up later."

"Who?" Rupert looked mystified. "Did you bring along another schoolmate to join our reunion?"

"Nothing like that," Basil said. With my help, he quickly explained the Alfie situation to Rupert. Then the three of us set out toward Ratcliffe.

Even being away for so long, my paws remembered the way to the sites of some of my fondest memories. Oxford had changed over the years, but not much. When we reached the circular Radcliffe Camera, Rupert led the way in through a crack in the stone exterior. Ratcliffe College looked much the same as I remembered.

We passed the chapel and the Faculty Club, the English department and the student lounge. Young scholarly looking mice scurried here and there, from classroom to dormitory, several of them bowing respectfully when they spotted Professor Kerr. For once, Basil attracted no attention. I found myself wondering if these high-minded mice, so focused on their studies of natural science or classical literature, even knew of the crime and mayhem that went on outside these hallowed halls!

I forgot about such questions when we passed the Ratcliffe Museum of Art and Antiquities—and Basil stopped short at its doors, nearly causing me to bump into him. "Ah, the museum!" Basil exclaimed. "I've heard about the visiting exhibit of Far Eastern Treasures currently on display. Perhaps we can find time to view it while we're here, Dawson."

"That sounds fine," I said. "But at the moment I'm more interested in seeing our chums—and perhaps a nice platter of cheese—than any antiquities!"

That made Rupert chuckle. "You always were a practical sort of fellow, Dawson," he said with a hearty clap on my shoulder. "Now let's continue—the others are eager to see you two as well!"

A few minutes later we reached the Ratcliffe Library, a spacious and sprawling place filled with books, musty smells, classical statuary—and, at the moment, old friends!

"Basil! Dawson!" a cry went up, and then we were surrounded.

I laughed as I clasped hands with one old pal after another. "Clive—Cedric—Cyril!" I exclaimed, greeting each in turn. "What a treat to have the C for Cheese Gang back together!"

That was what we'd called the trio back in our
university days, for it was how Cyril, a friendly
mouse with a quick sense of humor, had introduced
himself upon our very first meeting—"Hullo, chaps.
I'm Cyril—that's Cyril with a *c*, as in cheese!"

For a moment, everyone seemed to talk at once
as we asked after one another's health and homes.
But then Cedric turned eagerly to Rupert. "Did
you tell them yet?" he asked.

Clive gasped. "Yes, did you?" he cried, while
Cyril nodded, his tail twitching with interest.

"Tell us what?" Basil suddenly stood taller, his ears alert. I could tell he'd noted the gleam in all our friends' eyes, as had I.

"Yes, tell us what?" I asked.

Rupert merely smiled. "Not yet," he told the gang.

"Oh, I'll tell them!" Cyril whirled to face Basil and me. "The Ratcliffe Library is haunted!"

TALES OF THE
HAUNTED LIBRARY

"HAUNTED?" BASIL ECHOED WITH A SMIRK. "ALL right, then. What's the punch line to this joke, old friends?"

"No joke, Basil," Cedric said earnestly.

I glanced at Rupert, who was never one to believe in wild tales or superstitions, expecting him to laugh off what the C for Cheese Gang had just said. But he was pinching one whisker, looking uncertain.

"I'm not prepared to go that far," he told Basil and me. "But there have been several, er, unexplained occurrences recently. That's one of the reasons I was so eager for you to come, Basil—I thought you might be able to get to the bottom of things."

"I see." Basil nodded shortly. "What do you mean by 'unexplained occurrences'?"

"All sorts of terrible things!" Cyril spoke up. "Noises deep in the night . . ."

". . . broken statues," Clive continued, gesturing to an alcove in the wall nearby that held a chipped bust of some ancient mouse philosopher or poet. "Books being moved around without any mouse being responsible . . ."

". . . or disappearing entirely," Cedric added. His eyes widened. "Some say the place is haunted by the ghost of a past librarian, Whiskers the Wise." He pointed to one of several portraits hanging on the wall nearby—specifically one showing a stout, bespectacled older mouse with kind eyes.

Cyril nodded. "Whiskers is said to have sworn he would never leave his beloved library—not even after death!"

"Stuff and nonsense," Basil scoffed. "But vandalism is a serious matter. We need to get to the bottom of what's really going on."

"Exactly. Which is why you're the perfect fellow

for the job, Basil," Rupert told him. "Perhaps your scientific sleuthing methods can uncover the true cause of all the trouble."

I chuckled. "At least we can cross Ratigan off the suspect list this time," I joked to Basil. "After all, he was in prison until last night!"

Basil ignored my jest, peering around at the library with new interest. We were currently gathered in the front room, which contained mostly tables and seating for study and socializing. An arch at the back of this area led into the larger main room, where the stacks—the tall rows of shelves that held the library's large collection of books, parchments, and manuscripts—were located.

"Where has most of the trouble taken place?" Basil asked, stepping closer to the chipped statue and examining it closely.

Cyril shrugged. "All over, I think," he said. "Obviously the damaged statue is out here, and there have been reports of strange noises and sudden cold breezes throughout the library."

"Yes." Cedric looked toward the arch. "And of course the issues with the books occurred mostly in the stacks."

Clive tilted his head, his round ears swiveling. "Did any of you hear a noise just now?"

"What sort of noise?" I asked, having heard nothing but the sounds of our own voices.

"I think I heard it too," Rupert said. "Like a distant crash from somewhere in the stacks."

"We'd better go see," I said. I hurried toward the arch with Basil and the others at my heels.

When we got a look into the stacks, I gasped. A large bookcase was tipped over, and a mouse was sprawled on the floor nearby, unconscious!

5

A CLOSE CALL

"OH NO!" RUPERT CRIED, PUSHING PAST ME. "THAT'S Lewis, the head librarian!"

We all rushed to the fallen librarian's aid. "Stand back," Basil ordered. "Give him air and let Dawson have a look at him."

I knelt by the mouse's side, glad for my medical training at such a critical moment. Fortunately I could see immediately that Lewis's breath was strong and steady, and there was no sign of blood.

"Sir, can you hear me?" I asked, carefully reaching to feel his pulse.

Lewis let out a groan, and his eyes fluttered

open. "Wha—what happened?" he murmured, blinking rapidly several times.

"Easy—don't try to sit up until I can determine whether you've broken any bones," I said.

But the mouse ignored my order, pushing himself to a sitting position. "I think I'm all right," he said, his voice sounding stronger already. "The fall knocked the breath out of me, that's all."

Basil bent toward him. "Do you remember what happened?"

"I think so." Lewis glanced toward the fallen bookshelf. "I was merely walking past this area on my way to return a volume of poetry to its place on the shelves." His gaze shifted to a book lying nearby. "Suddenly I felt a cold breeze, as if someone had opened a window on an icy winter day—and then I heard an ominous creaking sound. I flung myself out of the way in the nick of time as the bookshelf came crashing down—onto the very spot where I'd been standing!"

"Oh dear!" Cedric exclaimed.

"Was it the ghost?" Clive wondered.

"Doubtful," Basil retorted. He stepped over to examine the bookshelf, clearly looking for clues.

I returned my attention to Lewis, checking him over carefully. But it seemed he had truly made a narrow escape and was unharmed, aside from being a bit shaken and pale.

Only when I was satisfied that my medical skills weren't needed did I turn to observe Basil. "Any clues?" I called to him.

Basil was bent over, peering closely at the bookshelf. "I can tell that you take good care of this library," he said to Lewis. "There's not a speck of dust on these shelves. Too bad, since that means no evidence of pawprints."

Clive looked confused. "What do you mean, 'pawprints'?"

"I'm referring, of course, to a new method of scientific crime-solving—one that Mr. Sherlock Holmes has pioneered." Basil tucked both hands behind his back and paced before us as he explained. "You see, each mouse's paw leaves its own unique print, just as each human hand leaves unique fingerprints. If a detective can match a print to a suspect . . ."

"Ah, I see!" Rupert looked impressed. "Very useful, I'm sure."

"I suppose so." Cyril shrugged. "But ghosts don't leave pawprints, do they?"

"Ghosts don't exist," Basil snapped. "So your question is moot!"

Rupert cleared his throat. "Let's leave poor Lewis to his recovery and move on, shall we?" he suggested tactfully. "I believe there's a fine meal awaiting us in the Faculty Club. . . ."

I was happy to tuck into the excellent dinner that was awaiting us in the wood-paneled club.

But Basil only picked at his food, seeming lost in thought as the rest of us reminisced about the last time we'd all met within these hallowed halls.

Finally talk turned to the mystery of the haunted library, and only then did Basil take an interest in our conversation. "There does seem to be something suspicious going on," I commented.

"Yes indeed." Basil picked up a scrap of Emmental cheese, staring at it for a moment before popping it into his mouth. "But I can assure you that ghosts are not behind it."

"Can you be sure, Basil?" Rupert sat back in his chair, smiling. "Many scholars might disagree."

Cyril nodded eagerly and leaned forward. "Yes, haven't you heard about the Ghost Club?"

"What's that?" I asked, helping myself to another chunk of Wensleydale.

"It's a human group, formed at Trinity College, Cambridge," Rupert said. He automatically wrinkled his nose at the mention of the competing university, as did the rest of us. "It's a place to discuss ghosts and other supernatural incidents. The late Charles Dickens himself was said to be a member."

"See, Basil?" Cedric said with a slight smirk.

"That proves that even the most intelligent and learned people—and mice—can believe in the possibility of the supernatural."

"It proves only that even the most intelligent and learned can be fools," Basil retorted. "Whatever has been happening in the library, it has nothing to do with the supernatural. And I'll prove it—if only to show you that mortal paws are surely behind it all!"

AFTER-DINNER SURPRISES

OUR WELCOME DINNER LASTED LATE INTO THE night as the six of us told stories, raised toasts, and ate endless quantities of fine cheese and other delicacies. As the clock struck midnight, Cedric pushed back from the table with a groan.

"I think I overdid it on the cheddar, chaps," he announced. "I'd best leave you to it and head off to bed."

I prepared to rise. "If you're not feeling well, someone should walk you home."

"No, no, please stay." Cedric put a paw on my shoulder to keep me in my chair. "It's just a touch of indigestion—a common malady for one like me,

who likes a bit too much of good food and drink!"
He chuckled. "Don't fret. I'll be ready to join you
for a hearty breakfast after a good night's sleep!"

With a wave, he took his leave. Rupert stood to
serve us each a bite of cheese. "We've just received
this excellent Halloumi from Cyprus—you all must
try it. . . ."

And thus we returned to our revelry. But all
parties must end eventually, and half an hour later

Cyril let out a prodigious yawn. "Oh dear," he said. "The journey to get here is catching up with me, I'm afraid. Shall we call it an evening?"

"Yes, I'm tired as well," Rupert said. "But I look forward to more of this fine company tomorrow!"

After a round of farewells, we parted ways outside the Faculty Club. Basil and I were staying in a spare apartment at the west end of campus beyond the library, while the C for Cheese Gang had lodgings near Rupert's regular quarters, which were only a block away.

It was quite late by then, with not a creature stirring as Basil and I strolled toward our temporary home. "That was fun, wasn't it?" I commented, stifling a slight burp. "It's good to have the old gang together again."

"Hmm." Basil didn't seem to be listening. He was walking along with his hands behind his back, eyes cast slightly upward and with a distant expression. I recognized the look well—he was deep in thought.

"Has your mind returned to our ghost?" I asked lightly.

Basil shot me an impatient look. "I am thinking about the case, yes," he said. "But please do not pretend you have the slightest belief in the ghost theory. You have more sense than that, Dawson."

I merely shrugged, not bothering to say that he was right—I had little belief in ghosts and other spirits. But it was rather fun to allow him to think I might!

We had nearly reached the Ratcliffe Museum by then. A guard stood outside, dressed in a smart uniform. When I took a closer look at him, I gasped.

"Why, look here," I exclaimed. "It's young Alfie from the train!"

Basil looked surprised. But there was no arguing with my comment, for it was indeed our young acquaintance. He smiled at us bashfully, tipping his cap.

"Hello again, Mr. Basil, Dr. Dawson," he said. "What are you two doing out and about at this hour, if you don't mind my asking?"

"We've just come from dinner," I said. "But what are you doing here? Have you found a job already?"

Alfie smiled and squared his shoulders. "As luck

would have it, two of the regular guards just quit, so I was hired on immediately!"

"How nice!" I said.

"Indeed," Basil agreed, though he still seemed a bit distracted.

Remembering how I'd been needling Basil about ghosts, I couldn't help winking and adding, "But be careful working so late at night, Alfie. Rumor has it there are ghosts about!"

Basil shot me an irritated look. But Alfie's eyes widened. "Ghosts? What do you mean, sir?"

"It's Basil's latest case," I told him with a smile. "There's been some minor mischief at the library, and our friends have been hearing stories about a ghostly librarian haunting the place. . . ."

"But you needn't worry," Basil told the young mouse, who was looking rather alarmed. "Ghosts don't exist—that's scientific fact. And now that I'm on the case, we'll soon discover who's really behind the trouble."

We bade good night to Alfie and continued on our way. The library stood just ahead, its narrow windows darkened and empty. This late at night, the grand old place certainly looked spooky enough to be haunted!

"Perhaps we should stop, Dawson," Basil said as he neared the library. "I've been thinking about that fallen bookcase, and I'd like to check on something."

"Can't your sleuthing wait until morning, Basil?" I complained with a yawn. "It's late, and I'm tired."

He opened his mouth as if to argue. But at that moment both of us were silenced by a sudden loud, otherworldly howl coming from inside the library!

7

INVESTIGATING
A GHOST

BASIL RUSHED FORWARD, REACHING THE DOORS before the howl had fully faded. I hesitated, chilled despite myself by the unearthly sound. When I glanced once more at the library windows, I gasped—for a pale face was peering out of one of them!

"Basil!" I cried. But when I blinked, the face disappeared! Had I really seen it? Or was it a side effect of too much rich food and too little sleep?

Basil didn't hear me. He was pushing into the library, which stood unlocked at all hours for students who might need it. "Show yourself!" he shouted, his voice echoing back to me from the

cavernous front room. "Who is here? Step forward at once!"

I shivered, feeling a cool breeze tickle my whiskers, even though there were few drafts this far inside the Radcliffe Camera's sturdy stone walls. "Basil!" I called. "Do you see anyone?"

Basil stepped outside. "Get in here and help me

search, Dawson," he ordered. "This could be our chance to catch our culprit red-pawed!"

I was in no hurry to rush into the darkened library in search of the source of that howl, though I wasn't eager to admit as much to Basil. Luckily, at that moment a much more ordinary shout went up from behind us. I turned and saw Rupert, Cyril, and Clive hurrying toward us.

"Basil! Dawson!" Rupert cried as he drew near, huffing and puffing from exertion. "What the dickens is all the hubbub?"

I was surprised to see them, though certainly not unhappy to have reinforcements arrive. "We heard a noise from inside," I said, waving a paw at the library.

"What sort of noise?" Clive asked.

Basil peered at him. "But surely you heard it yourselves?" he asked rather sharply. "Otherwise, why would you be rushing this way instead of tucked into your beds?"

The trio exchanged a confused look. "The only noise we heard was you shouting, Basil," Rupert said.

Clive nodded. "We'd stopped to continue our

conversation outside Rupert's place," Cyril explained. "In the quiet night, we heard you cry out . . ."

". . . and naturally, we rushed to see what was the matter," Clive finished with a shrug.

"But didn't you hear the—the howl before that?" I queried. "It sounded like . . . like . . ." I paused, my powers of description failing me.

"Like a ghost?" Cyril widened his eyes.

"Not at all," Basil snapped. "It sounded much like someone *pretending* to be a ghost, however."

Clive shivered visibly. "Are you certain of that?" he asked, casting a nervous look at the library. "What if the ghost librarian knows that you're investigating—and he doesn't like it?"

Rupert was staring at the library, stroking his whiskers thoughtfully. "Perhaps we should take a look inside? The scoundrel might still be lurking about," he suggested.

"Doubtful." Basil shook his head, seeming to have lost all interest in rushing inside to investigate. "Whoever made that noise has surely escaped by now while we stand here engaged in endless silly chitchat."

He sounded irritated, and I hoped our friends wouldn't take offense. "Never mind," I said with forced cheer. "It's late, eh? Let's discuss it further in the morning."

AT THE
MUSEUM

WHEN I OPENED MY EYES THE NEXT MORNING, still weary from the night of revelry, Basil was fully awake, fully dressed, and bustling around our quarters.

"Hop to, Dawson," he said when he saw I was awake. "I was thinking this morning is the perfect time to visit the exhibit."

"The exhibit?" I echoed with a yawn.

"The visiting exhibit of Far Eastern Treasures at the museum, Dawson," Basil said. "Have you forgotten already? I said I hoped to take it in during this visit."

I sat up and rubbed my eyes with both paws.

"All right, Basil." I was surprised that he wasn't eager to get started immediately on the library mystery, but I was too tired to ask why.

When we entered the exhibit hall a short while later, I felt more awake at once. The Far Eastern Treasures were spectacular! Porcelain vases and silk

tapestries, glittering jewels and painted fans and intricately etched teapots—everywhere I looked, I saw the most exotic objects imaginable.

"I'm glad we came, Basil!" I exclaimed, pausing to examine a platter painted with peacocks and palm fronds. "I wouldn't have wanted to miss seeing such a collection of valuables! It almost makes me forget about the ghost."

I expected him to object, as usual, to my implication that the ghost might be real. Instead, he merely looked thoughtful. "I've been pondering the case, Dawson," he said, strolling on toward the next display. "Clearly there's a living mouse—or mice—behind the shenanigans at the library. But what is the motive?"

"Are you absolutely sure it's a living mouse?" I countered. "What if there really is a ghost? The occurrences seem to match with what I've read of hauntings—the cold breezes coming seemingly from nowhere, the minor damage and unearthly sounds and sights. . . ."

Basil sighed loudly. "Dawson, please do not waste my time with that nonsense," he said. "Surely you've been observing me—and Mr. Holmes—for

long enough to know that there's always a logi-
cal explanation for mysterious happenings. The
spooky sounds could easily be made by a living
mouse. And the damage is nothing that mortal
paws couldn't manage."

"Are you sure? That bookcase looked quite
heavy. And the cold spots . . ."

But Basil was no longer listening. He stared at
a display of glazed bowls, though he hardly seemed
to see them. "Perhaps a mouse intent on thievery
is trying to frighten away the gullible," he mused
aloud. "The culprit could be after the library's
rare-book collection, perhaps, or some of its more
valuable statuary. . . ."

"Really, Basil?" Now it was my turn to sound
dubious. "Who would bother putting so much
effort into pilfering that sort of thing when *this*
lies right beneath their whiskers?" I swept an arm
around to indicate the museum exhibit.

Basil shrugged. "This museum is well guarded,
and locked up tightly at night," he reminded me.
"The library, on the other paw, is open night and
day—and often quite deserted in the wee hours."

We continued to discuss the case as we

wandered through the rest of the exhibit. Finally having satisfied our taste for eastern treasures, we left the museum. Just outside, we found Alfie on duty once again.

"Working hard, I see, eh, lad?" I said with a friendly clap on his shoulder.

"Yes. I went home shortly after I saw you last and resumed duty again just now. I'm glad for as many hours as possible, Dr. Dawson," Alfie replied with his customary tip of the cap.

"You'll be able to afford Ratcliffe's tuition sooner than expected at this rate, I'll wager," I commented.

Alfie smiled and glanced bashfully at the ground. "Yes, I suppose so."

"Look, Dawson." Basil nodded at something behind me. "Here comes Rupert."

When I turned, our friend had nearly reached us. He had a smile on his face and a newspaper tucked beneath his arm.

"May I see that, please?" Basil snatched the paper without awaiting an answer. "I've been wondering if there's any progress in recapturing Ratigan."

"Not yet I'm afraid, old chum," Rupert said. "The police in London are stumped."

"Begging your pardon, sirs," Alfie spoke up. "Some of the other museum employees were talking about Professor Ratigan when I arrived this morning. The rumor is that he has already left London bound for Amsterdam—one of the fellows has a cousin who saw him at the channel crossing!"

"Really? That's good news, eh, Basil?" I elbowed my friend.

Basil shrugged. "Not for the mice of Amsterdam," he said. "But I suppose it does give me enough time to solve our little Ratcliffe mystery before I set off to Amsterdam to track him down."

MORE MYSTERIOUS MATTERS

AFTER A PLEASANT LUNCH WITH OUR FRIENDS, Basil and I headed to the library to look for clues. A handful of students were gathered in the front room, reading or scribbling notes or chatting softly. We paid them little mind, continuing straight on into the main room. Lewis was at the librarian's desk, though he hurried to greet us the moment we crossed the threshold.

"I'm so glad you're back!" he cried. "Professor Kerr says you're looking into what happened— well, there's been more trouble!"

"Already?" I exclaimed, thinking back to the unearthly howl the previous night and the toppled bookcase a few hours before that.

"What happened?" Basil asked. "Tell me everything—omit no detail, for anything might turn out to be important."

Lewis nodded, wringing his paws. "Where to begin?" he said with a sigh. "When I arrived this morning, I found those chairs moved. . . ." He nodded to indicate three chairs crammed into a corner. "Several books had been knocked from their shelves. And as I looked at them, I heard the bell on my desk ringing as if to summon me—but when I hurried back here, there was no mouse in sight!"

"Oh dear!" I exclaimed. "What do you think, Basil?"

The great detective had already stepped over to examine the chairs. "Where are the fallen books?" he asked Lewis.

The librarian shrugged. "I returned them to their normal spots, so as not to allow them to become further damaged," he said. "I'm sorry. Was that wrong?"

"If anything else happens, touch nothing until I've been here," Basil instructed him sternly. "You

might inadvertently disturb some clue that could reveal the identity of the culprit."

"Do ghosts leave clues?" Lewis wondered, his voice and whiskers trembling slightly.

Basil scoffed. "Surely a mouse of letters such as yourself has no true belief in ghosts, sir!"

"I didn't think so." Lewis shook his head. "But Dr. Kerr is so knowledgeable about all things ghostly— if he thinks it's possible, who am I to argue?"

"Rupert knows a lot about ghosts?" I asked in surprise. "I wouldn't think that would fall among his interests."

Lewis shrugged. "Well, I suppose a learned mouse such as himself takes an interest in everything. . . ."

Basil just let out a soft harrumph, his sharp eyes darting to another part of the room. "I see someone has returned that bookcase to its upright position," he said.

"Yes, several strong students helped me take care of that first thing this morning," the librarian said. "I didn't want it to be in the way."

"I see." Basil wandered toward the bookcase, which I could now hardly tell from its mates. He stopped near it, bending down to examine the wooden floor.

"Are there pawprints, Basil?" I asked, for I recalled other instances in which a stray print had been the clue he needed to solve a case.

"Of course not, Dawson," he replied rather sharply. "And if there were, I could only assume they belonged to Lewis or the students he just mentioned."

I shrugged, knowing better than to ask more questions when Basil took that sort of tone. While he continued his examination of the floor, I questioned Lewis a bit more about the latest occurrences, though he had little to add to what he'd already told us.

As we were chatting, there was a muffled crash from somewhere farther back in the stacks. "Oh dear!" Lewis cried, leaping to attention.

Basil was on the alert at once. "Is anyone else back there?" he barked at the librarian.

"No—not a soul." Lewis rushed past us into the stacks. "I haven't seen anyone aside from the two of you go back there. It sounded as if it came from this direction. . . ."

He led the way through the mazelike warren of

tall shelves. Finally we rounded a corner—and saw
that the entire contents of a large bookshelf had
fallen higgledy-piggledy to the floor!

"Stop!" Basil ordered, holding out an arm to
keep Lewis and me from moving any closer to the
crime scene. "I want to look for clues."

He took several moments to look around carefully. Then he waved us forward.

"I'm finished," he told Lewis. "You may clean
this up now if you'd like."

"Thank you." Lewis knelt beside the pile and
picked up one volume. "At least these aren't among
the more valuable books in the collection," he said
with a sigh.

"Of course not," I said with a grin. "The ghost is
a librarian too, remember? He must still care about
books, eh?"

10

EN ROUTE

LEAVING LEWIS TO HIS WORK, BASIL AND I
LEFT the library and strolled through the bustling campus toward the Faculty Club. Rupert
had told us that a big reunion dinner was planned
there that evening—not only he and the C for
Cheese Gang would be in attendance, but many
other beloved friends and faculty members, as well.
I was looking forward to it immensely, though I
worried that Basil might be too distracted by the
newest developments in our ghostly mystery to
enjoy it fully.

"Have you reached any conclusions about the

case yet, Basil?" I asked. "I'm sure our friends will be curious when we see them again."

Basil glanced at me. "As a matter of fact, I do have a theory," he told me with a slight smirk. "But I'm not prepared to discuss it just yet."

"What do you mean?" I was surprised—and perhaps even a little hurt. After all, I had been Basil's confidant and sounding board for many years, and many cases.

"I mean what I just said." Basil shrugged and stuck both paws in his pockets. "I don't wish to discuss it at the moment."

I dodged a student rushing past with his snout buried in a book. "But wouldn't you rather get my input now?" I said to Basil. "As I mentioned, you will surely be asked about it at dinner."

"I suppose I might, and I'm sure I'll have an answer at that time," Basil said with infuriating calmness. "But at this time, I have nothing to say."

I frowned, growing more irritated by the moment. "I hope you've come up with something more than your determination that ghosts don't exist," I snapped. "Because I watched you look for clues, and I didn't see a thing!"

"Didn't you?" Basil still sounded calm—and still wore that infuriating smirk. "I see."

"Good afternoon, Mr. Basil, Dr. Dawson."

I didn't realize we'd reached the museum until Alfie greeted us. He was on duty still, dressed in his smart guard's uniform.

"Good afternoon, Alfie," Basil said. "Don't mind us—Dawson is feeling a bit argumentative at the moment."

"I am not!" I protested. "I was only asking you to talk about the case, as we've done thousands of time before!"

"The case?" Alfie looked interested. "Do you mean the ghost in the library?"

"Indeed," Basil replied. Then he stepped toward the young mouse, leaned closer, and whispered something in his ear. Alfie's eyes widened, and he nodded and tipped his hat to Basil.

"What was that?" I asked sharply. "I didn't hear what you said to our young friend, Basil."

"You weren't meant to." Basil nodded to Alfie and set off again down the walkway.

I scurried to catch up. "What the blazes is going on, Basil?" I exclaimed. "You're acting most exasper-ating! Why won't you tell me what you're thinking?"

"Better safe than sorry, old friend," Basil told me as he strode onward. "But don't fret—all will become clear soon enough. . . ."

11
REVELRIES AND REVELATIONS

AS OUR REUNION CELEBRATION BEGAN, I CONTINUED to fume a bit over Basil's behavior. But the outstanding cheese puff appetizers helped soothe my spirits a bit, as did the congenial company of so many old friends. By the time the second course was served, I'd nearly forgotten about the library ghost.

Then one of our old professors of natural science turned to Basil with a curious expression. "Basil, old chum," he began. "Rupert tells me you're investigating the strange goings-on at the library. Have you figured out what is happening?"

I wasn't the only mouse who heard the question.

Most of the other diners turned to listen for the great detective's response.

Basil paused, glancing around with a slight smile. "As a matter of fact, I have been giving the matter quite a bit of attention," he told the professor and the rest of us. "And through the use of scientific sleuthing—and a bit of common sense—I have solved the case."

A gasp went up from all around. "You have?" Rupert cried.

"Did you trap the ghost?" Cedric asked.

Basil took a sip of his drink. "This was one of the more . . . interesting cases of my career," he said after a moment. "It made me look at things in a whole new way."

My eyes widened. What was Basil saying? Had he really changed his mind about ghosts?

"What are you talking about, Basil?" Rupert asked. "What did you figure out, exactly?"

"I'm not sure I can do it justice merely by telling you my conclusions." Basil looked around the table. "I'd prefer to show you—at the library itself. We can go right after dinner."

Clive pushed back his chair. "The rest of our dinner can wait," he declared. "But I can't wait another moment to hear your conclusions about our library ghost!"

"Agreed!" Rupert stood as well. "Come along, gang—the staff can keep the rest of our meal warm until we return."

There was a general murmur of agreement. Before I knew it, we were all hurrying out of the Faculty Club and along the walkway. It was getting late, and not many mice were around, which was probably a good thing, as I fear our group was rather raucous, joking loudly about ghosts and other matters.

As we walked, the others continued to pepper Basil with questions. But he refused to say a word, merely striding along with a gentle smirk on his face.

I knew better than to try to get him to speak before he was ready. So I just walked along with the others. When we passed the museum, the doors were closed and locked, and no mouse was in view outside. It seemed whichever mouse had taken over after Alfie's shift wasn't as diligent about his job as our young friend from the train!

Soon after that, we reached the library, which

stood open and welcoming as always. Basil led the way inside, straight back to the main room. Lewis had long since gone home for the evening, and the librarian's big old desk was unmoused. Basil leaned against it and looked around at us, his audience.

"Well?" Cyril asked, sounding impatient. "Will you tell us your conclusion now, Basil? Or must we guess?"

"Oh, that wouldn't be fair." Basil's smile widened. "Most of you would never be able to guess who was behind the mischief. But for others, it might be a bit too easy."

"What are you on about, Basil?" I was feeling impatient myself by now, especially when I remembered the tasty food still waiting for us back at the club. "Tell us what you've concluded, please."

"Fine." Basil stood up straight. "You'll all be happy to know that there is no ghost haunting this library."

"But you said . . . ," Clive began. He, Cedric, and Cyril were standing at the front of the group beside Rupert.

Basil raised a paw for silence. "No, as I've

maintained all along, the mischief all came at the paws of living mice. Specifically—you!"

With that, he pointed to Rupert and the C for Cheese Gang!

12

A STARTLING DISCOVERY

I GASPED. "BASIL, WHAT ARE YOU SAYING?" I CRIED.

Cyril puffed out his chest. "How dare you accuse us!" he exclaimed.

"Why, I never!" Cedric added, fanning himself with one paw.

But Rupert laughed and rolled his eyes. "Never mind, gang," he said. "I told you he'd figure it out! That means you each owe me a pound of fine cheese!" He pointed at Cyril, Clive, and Cedric in turn before returning his attention to Basil. "Yes, Basil, it was us."

"Quite a good prank to play on a world-famous

detective, eh, old chap?" Clive added, sounding pleased with himself.

"I thought he might be falling for it," Cedric said.

Cyril chuckled. "I was half-convinced of the ghost's existence myself!"

"Wait—you four set this up yourselves?" I exclaimed.

Basil peered at me. Then he nodded, seeming satisfied by something. "Ah, then you weren't in on it, Dawson? I hope you'll forgive me for my earlier secrecy. I couldn't be sure, and didn't want you to alert the others that I'd figured out the truth."

I nodded slowly, understanding now why Basil had refused to tell me anything earlier. He'd suspected I might be involved in the prank!

Rupert clapped me on the back. "No, Dawson wasn't involved—just the four of us." He gestured again toward the C for Cheese Gang. "I've taken an interest in the supernatural lately—merely scholarly, of course. When I mentioned as much to Cedric, he was sure Basil would scoff at my wasting time studying such matters."

"Right." Cyril grinned. "And that gave me the idea for the wager."

"Cyril, Cedric, and I thought we could convince Basil that the library was haunted," Clive went on.

"And Rupert thought Basil would see through our charade and solve the mystery as he's solved so many others," Cyril finished. "It seems he was correct!"

"But how did you figure it out, Basil?" Cedric asked.

"Yes, we were so careful!" Clive said.

Rupert smiled. "You certainly can't accuse me of not playing my part to the hilt," he commented to the C for Cheese Gang.

"No indeed—you were quite masterful," Cedric agreed with a little bow of respect.

"We even convinced Lewis to help us," Cyril added. "He didn't give us away, did he?"

"Not at all—Lewis played his part quite masterfully as well." Basil leaned against the desk again. "However, his near miss with the fallen bookcase was the main clue."

"How do you mean?" someone asked. The entire group was gathered around listening, even though a few mice looked a bit confused.

"It could have been a stroke of luck that Lewis wasn't badly hurt when the bookcase toppled," Basil explained. "However, it would take more than luck for the heavy wooden bookcase to avoid damaging the wooden floor when it fell!"

I gasped, suddenly recalling the careful way Basil had examined the floor. I'd thought he was looking for pawprints, but he was searching for scratches!

"You caught us," Rupert said with a chuckle. "Lewis promised to play along—but only if we didn't cause any real damage to his library."

Cyril nodded, waving a paw toward the stacks.

"It took five volunteer students to tip over that heavy bookcase without dropping it!"

"How could we have known that action in itself would give us away?" Clive exclaimed.

Basil smiled. "Oh, don't worry. That wasn't the only thing," he said. "I couldn't help but notice that Cedric left dinner early last night—and that the other three of you showed up just in time to witness us hearing that strange howl."

Cedric grinned. "You mean this howl?" With that, he let out a piercing yowl that made several of the other listeners move a few steps away.

After that, the conspirators explained the rest of the spooky pieces of the puzzle. They had simply made up the stories they'd told us upon arrival, of course. But it had been Cedric's face I'd spotted in the window right after the howl. And Clive had been the one who'd been hidden deep in the stacks to push those books off the shelf earlier in the day.

Then I remembered a detail that hadn't been addressed. "What about the cold breeze?" I asked.

Cyril shrugged. "We told Lewis to say that," he said.

"Yes," Rupert agreed. "It's well known that

ghostly visitors are meant to bring with them a sudden spot of cold air."

"No, not the one Lewis mentioned," I said. "I felt it myself—a sudden, unexplained cold breeze outside the library last night."

Basil chuckled. "I suspect that might be attributed to your own active imagination, Dawson. After all, you seemed more than ready to believe in ghosts!"

I frowned slightly. Could he be right? Had I imagined the chill tickling my fur as I stood on the deserted walkway outside the library?

Before I could figure it out, there was a shout from nearby. One of our other old classmates had wandered over to look at some of the books on one of the wooden bookcases and was pointing to the floor at the bottom of the case.

"Are you sure ghosts aren't real?" he cried. "Because there are glowing pawprints back here!"

We all rushed to see. Sure enough, several eerie, glowing prints marred the floor! I gulped, flashing back to the unexplained cold breeze I'd felt. Could ghosts be real after all?

Our old natural sciences professor let out a

gasp when he got a look. "Stand back!" he cried. "It's phosphorus!"

"Phosphorus?" Rupert looked around at the C for Cheese Gang. "But we agreed not to risk using that, even though it would look terribly ghostly!"

Cedric nodded. "White phosphorus is far too unstable—that's why most educated people no longer use the cheap matches made from it. It's so dangerously flammable that even the slightest friction can set it alight," he said. "Step back, everyone!"

We all rushed to obey. But someone moved too quickly, knocking a book off the shelf—right onto the phosphorescent prints.

Immediately, the book burst into flames!

FIRE!

ONE OF THE GREAT IRONIES OF LIFE IS THAT WHEN one is attempting to light a campfire or a cigar, it seems nearly impossible to convince the flame to take hold. But when one wishes *not* to burn something, fire can seem hungrier than any cat at the sight of a mouse.

"Oh no!" Cyril cried. "It's spreading to the shelf!"

He was correct. Tongues of flame darted out from the original book, licking at the wooden floor and bookshelf. Before any of us could react, several more books were on fire.

"Do something!" Cedric cried.

Rupert leaped forward, trying to smother the

flames with his jacket. But he succeeded only in setting one of the sleeves ablaze.

"We need water!" someone exclaimed.

There was a hubbub of shouts and rushing around as everyone tried to find something to douse the flames. I found myself knocked nearly off my feet by Clive as he stampeded past in search of help.

As I leaned briefly against a bookshelf, catching my breath after the shove, a faint voice tickled my ears: *"Behind the desk,"* it said.

I blinked, wondering if the shove had affected my mind and caused me to hallucinate.

Then it came again, more urgently this time: *"Behind the desk!"*

I pushed myself upright and rushed toward the librarian's desk. When I skidded around it, I gasped.

"Over here!" I shouted. "There's a big bucket of water—help me lift it!"

I grabbed the mop that was standing in the bucket and tossed it aside. By then, Cyril had arrived to help. The two of us hoisted the heavy bucket and carried it over to the fire. It was spreading fast, and for a moment I despaired, fearing we were too late. But Cyril was counting down—"Three, two, one, go!"—and I did my part, helping him splash the contents of the bucket over the burning books.

There was a great sizzling and hissing, and black smoke burst upward as the water doused the flames. A few books were still burning at the edges, but we were able to grab those, toss them onto the floor, and stomp out the rest of the fire.

"Whew!" Cedric exclaimed, mopping his brow. "That was close."

Rupert nodded and looked around. "With all these books and wooden shelves, the whole library could've gone up in flames before long!"

"The whole campus!" Clive pointed out. "What was to stop it from spreading?"

"It's lucky we were here," someone else called out.

Cyril snorted. "If we hadn't been here, the fire wouldn't have started," he pointed out.

"Maybe not now," the natural sciences professor countered. "But anything could've set off that phosphorus. As Cedric mentioned, it's terribly unstable."

"Yes." Rupert nodded grimly. "Which is why we'd agreed not to use it in our prank, tempting as it might have been." He looked around. "None of us went back on that, did we?"

"Not me!" Clive exclaimed, while Cedric and Cyril added their own assurances that they hadn't been the purveyors of the pawprints.

"Then where did those prints come from?" someone wondered.

I shrugged. "Perhaps Basil has a theory for . . ." I allowed my words to trail off as I glanced around and saw no sign of my friend. "Basil?"

14

TRACKING
BASIL

THE OTHERS STARTED LOOKING AROUND TOO. "Where'd Basil go?" Rupert asked.

"Perhaps he's out looking for more help," someone suggested.

I frowned. "It's not like Basil to go missing when trouble is afoot," I said. "If he's gone, he must have had an urgent reason to leave."

"But what could be more urgent than a fire?" Cyril wondered.

I glanced around, then smiled. "Aha!" I exclaimed, pointing at a set of wet pawprints leading toward the door. "If we follow those, I suspect we'll find out."

Rupert smiled. "Well done, Dawson."

"I haven't been the best friend and constant companion of the world's greatest detective all these years for nothing." I grinned, but it faded quickly as I returned to wondering where Basil had gone. "Now let's follow them!"

I took the lead, keeping my gaze on the wet pawprints on the clean wooden floor. They led through the archway, across the front room, and out the door. Outside, it was darker and a bit harder to see, but I was able to follow the prints as they turned and headed down the walkway.

And soon it wasn't necessary to follow the pawprints any longer, as I spotted the mouse who'd left them. Basil was just ahead, outside the museum's front doors—locked in paw-to-paw combat with two other mice!

I gasped as I recognized both of Basil's adversaries, each of them surprising in a different way. For one of them was Alfie, who had seemed so friendly, meek, and mild but who was now punching at Basil like a wild thing.

And the second . . . was Professor Ratigan!

Basil's old nemesis let out a shout as he saw

us coming. "Quickly, away!" he yelled at Alfie. "Hurry!"

Basil glanced around and saw us too. "Help me stop them!" he cried to us. "They're trying to steal the treasures!"

I gasped as I looked where he was pointing and saw boxes, bags, and crates set upon a hand truck. "Quickly!" I yelled to the others as I sprinted forward.

Alfie gave Basil one last shove, then darted away and grabbed a bag stuffed with what appeared to be ancient tapestries. Then he took off down the walkway.

"Not so fast!" cried Clive, who had been an excellent amateur hurdler in our university days. Apparently, he hadn't lost all of his speed, for he soon caught up to and tackled Alfie, who went down with a grunt, the tapestries spilling out onto the ground.

"Guard the valuables!" someone shouted. "Don't let them make off with anything else!"

Several of our friends gathered around the handcart. Basil strode toward Ratigan, who now stood sneering nearby.

"You might as well give yourself up, Ratigan," Basil said. "There's no way you can elude all of us."

Ratigan looked around at us. Then he smirked. "Are you sure about that, Basil?" he said.

Quick as a wink, he pulled something out of his cloak. I gasped when I saw what it was—a pair of white phosphorus matches!

"You!" I cried. "Basil, Ratigan must have left those prints in the library."

"Keep up, Dawson," Basil said grimly. "Ratigan, don't you dare—"

He didn't have a chance to finish. Ratigan scraped the matches against each other. As they

burst into flames, he tossed one at the pile of valuables—and the other straight at Basil!

There was a moment of frenzy as most of our group stomped out the fire before it could set any of the valuables alight. Meanwhile, Rupert, Cyril, and I rushed to Basil, helping him rip off his jacket and stomp out the flame that was already turning the fine tweed fabric to ash.

"Never mind my coat!" Basil cried. "Stop him—stop Ratigan!"

But by then it was already too late. Ratigan was gone—and though we immediately launched a search, he was nowhere to be found on campus.

15

HURRAH, HURRAH!

LATER, WE ALL GATHERED BACK IN THE FACULTY Club to finish our meal and discuss the night's adventures. Basil explained that he'd suspected young Alfie all along of being up to no good.

"But how?" I exclaimed as I helped myself to a bit of crumbly Greek Feta. "He seemed so nice on the train."

"Indeed." Basil nodded. "But he showed a bit too much interest in Ratigan's escape, not to mention knowledge of my own sleuthing exploits."

Rupert chuckled. "You must be used to that by now, Basil," he said. "Many mice the world over follow your exploits with all the raptness with which they might read a favorite novel by Mr. Dickens or Mr. Thackeray."

"Perhaps so." A shadow of a smile crossed Basil's face. "Nevertheless, it seemed odd that a poor church mouse would have such immediate knowledge of certain details about Ratigan's escape from prison only hours earlier . . . unless that mouse was actually Ratigan's accomplice!"

I gasped, remembering the newspaper headline: RATIGAN AND ACCOMPLICE ESCAPE NEWGATE PRISON. I also recalled Alfie telling us that it had taken the guards several hours to notice the escape. He'd claimed to have overheard that information at the train station—but now it seemed that had been a lie to cover his slip of the tongue. I hadn't thought much about it at the time, but then again, I wasn't a world-famous detective—merely the best friend of one.

"Did you really guess that so quickly, Basil?" I asked.

"Perhaps not," Basil replied. "But as I said, I had my suspicions that the lad was up to something. Especially when he mentioned the great fortune and coincidence of not one but two museum guards having so recently quit, vacating the job just when he appeared to ask for it."

"You mean Ratigan was behind that?" Cyril asked.

Basil nodded. "I expect when we track down the original guards, we'll find that they were bribed or threatened into quitting."

"That way Ratigan could install his accomplice, Alfie, in the job so it would be easier to figure out a way to abscond with the treasures," I said. "Brilliant reasoning, Basil!"

"But it must have confounded him when he learned from young Alfie that you were so close on the scene, Basil," Rupert added.

"I expect so." Basil shrugged with his usual lack of false modesty. "That must be why he didn't strike more immediately."

Clive shook his head. "Even so, it was a risk for him to attempt that heist with you around."

"Yes, I'm surprised he didn't simply wait until you'd departed back to London," Cedric said.

"I expect he planned to do exactly that." Basil speared a chunk of cheddar from the platter in the center of the table, examining it thoughtfully. "That's why I decided to bring things to a head— by whispering to young Alfie about our plans for this evening, including my plan to lead everyone to the library from our dinner."

I gasped again, this time recalling the way Basil had stopped to whisper something into Alfie's ear on our way to dinner. At the time, I'd been resentful toward my friend for keeping secrets. But now I realized he'd had a plan in mind all along!

"So in that way, you let Alfie—and thus Ratigan—know exactly where you would be, and when," I said. "They would have been hidden inside the museum, waiting to see us march past on our way to the library. Knowing we would be busy for the next few minutes at least, they would then take advantage of the perfect moment for their heist. . . ."

"Which I planned to interrupt." Basil grimaced. "However, I failed to take into account Ratigan's extra insurance plan—to plant those phosphorescent prints, keeping us busy saving the library from fiery destruction."

Clive looked up from his soup. "Alfie was sneering about that when we were dragging him off to the constable," he said. "He said Ratigan was proud of that trick, since he thought we'd all gone ghost-crazy—including Basil. He seemed to relish the idea of making Basil look foolish with his phony phosphorescent pawprints."

I smiled fondly at my old friend. "Not much chance of that," I commented. "Basil was one step ahead of the rest of us—as always."

"Hear! Hear!" Rupert raised his glass, and the others did likewise, toasting Basil's cleverness and diligence.

Cedric chuckled. "We should have known you'd never fall for our ghostly escapades, Basil."

"Indeed you should have," Basil replied. "I know better than to believe in silly tales good only for scaring small children."

I hesitated, wondering if I should mention the faint voice that had guided me toward the librarian's desk during the fire. No other mouse had been close enough to whisper in my ear. Besides that, none of our group had any way of knowing about that hidden bucket of water. So who had really sent me to fetch it—thus saving the library?

A sudden image flashed through my mind—a scholarly looking older mouse, spectacles sliding down his nose and books tucked beneath one stout arm. Just like the portrait of Whiskers the Wise on the library wall. I shivered, thinking back to

that whispery voice, that strangely chilly breeze tickling my fur. Could it be . . . ?

Meanwhile, Basil didn't seem as pleased as he might have been by the accolades. "One thing didn't go according to plan," he said. "Ratigan remains at large."

"Oh, I'm sure you'll take care of that soon enough." Rupert reached for another cracker. "At least you've thwarted his current criminal plans."

I nodded. "He's sure to make a mistake soon enough—criminals always do. Isn't that what you always tell me, Basil?"

He allowed that it was, indeed, a common comment from him. "It's one of the principles I learned from Mr. Holmes," he added. "And you're right, of course. I'll make sure Ratigan ends up where he belongs—back in prison with Alfie!"

"That's right," Rupert said. "In the meantime, the library and the museum exhibit are saved. . . ."

"The ghost mystery is solved . . . ," Cyril continued.

I smiled. "And it's time to relax and celebrate

a fine reunion—and an even finer dinner—with a very fine group of mice!"

This time we all lifted our glasses, with Basil leading us in a chorus of "Hurrah, Ratcliffe! Hurrah, hurrah!"